SPIDER-MAN

THE SUPER SPIDER

by
David Seidman
Illustrated by
Louie De Martinis

Meredith® Books
Des Moines, Iowa

ISBN 0-696-22516-6

Peter Parker was in a hurry. His friends saw him and shouted, "Hey, Peter! Slow down!"

"Sorry, guys," Peter answered. "It's the first day of class. I don't want to be late."

Peter's friends laughed. Why was Peter so eager to see the old professor?

The professor taught a class on spiders, but hardly anyone took the class. People joked that she liked spiders better than people.

Peter didn't mind. *This class should be easy,* he thought. *After all, I'm Spider-Man. I know all about being a spider. The professor will love me!*

"Some people take this class because they like Spider-Man," a raspy voice snarled, "and they think spiders are 'cool.' If that's you, get out now." It was the professor.

Her harsh words startled Peter. He blurted out, "What's wrong with Spider-Man?"

"Spider-Man," the professor growled, "doesn't deserve to call himself a spider. Some real spiders can handle heat that would cook a man. Can Spider-Man do that?"

"Well . . . no," Peter gulped. "But—"

"Some real spiders have fangs inject poison," the professor ed. She touched the picture of the der's fangs as if it were a beloved d. "Can Spider-Man do that?"

'No," Peter said. "But—"

"No buts!" the professor shouted. "Most real spiders have eight eyes, and some spiders can see in light too dim for people. In fact, they can see better in the dark than in the light. Can Spider-Man do that?"

"No, but—"

"Not another word," the professor said, scowling.

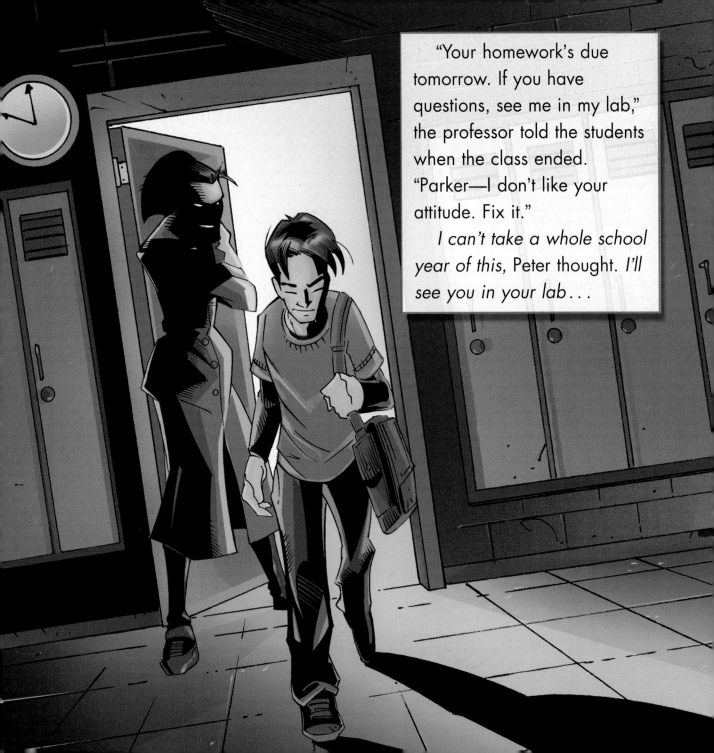

"Your homework's due tomorrow. If you have questions, see me in my lab," the professor told the students when the class ended. "Parker—I don't like your attitude. Fix it."

I can't take a whole school year of this, Peter thought. *I'll see you in your lab...*

. . . as Spider-Man! Maybe if she meets Spidey and I show her that Spidey's not such a bad guy, she won't be so mad at me for talking about him, Peter reasoned.

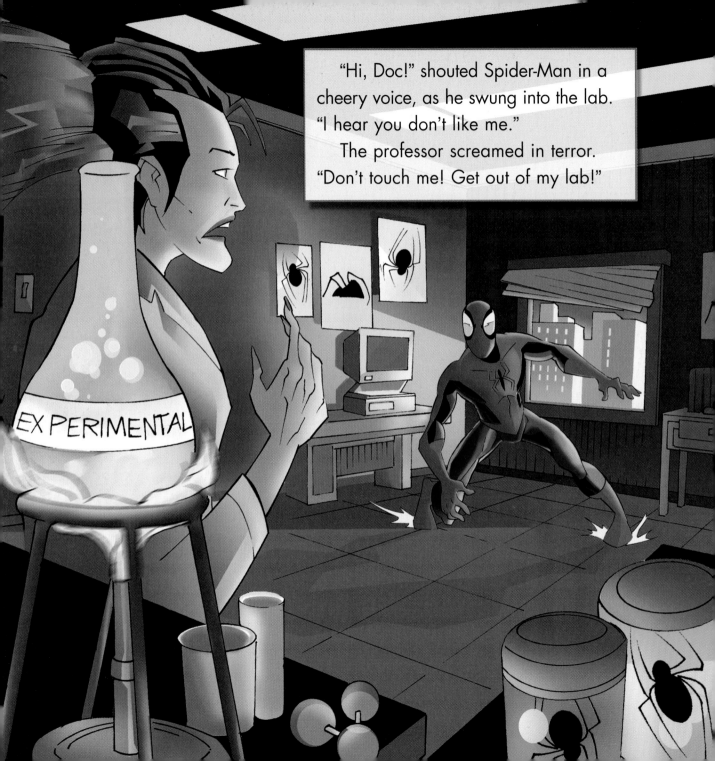

"Hi, Doc!" shouted Spider-Man in a cheery voice, as he swung into the lab. "I hear you don't like me."

The professor screamed in terror. "Don't touch me! Get out of my lab!"

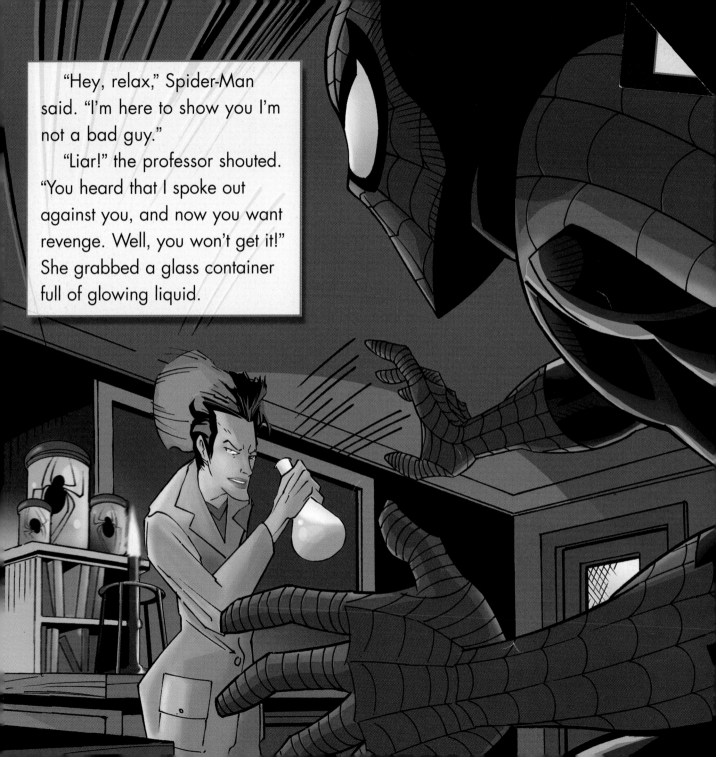

"Hey, relax," Spider-Man said. "I'm here to show you I'm not a bad guy."

"Liar!" the professor shouted. "You heard that I spoke out against you, and now you want revenge. Well, you won't get it!" She grabbed a glass container full of glowing liquid.

"Don't drink that stuff!" Spider-Man shouted. "Don't you see it's experimental? It's not safe!"

"I know. I made it," the professor said, and she drank the liquid.

Her skin darkened and hardened. Thick, hairy limbs poked from her sides. Her two eyes turned into eight.

To Spider-Man's shock, the professor had turned herself into a superhuman spider!

"You get famous," she hissed, "while almost nobody comes to my class on real spiders. It's not fair. But they'll pay attention to real spiders when I show what a real spider can do."

With one of her long legs, the professor-spider turned the lights off.

"Spiders like me can see well in the dark," she gloated, wrapping her legs around him, "but you can't."

Spider-Man tried to pull the professor-spider's legs off, but they were too strong. Suddenly, something felt wrong to Spider-Man. The professor's legs were tightening their grip, but that wasn't the problem. Something new was heading his way.

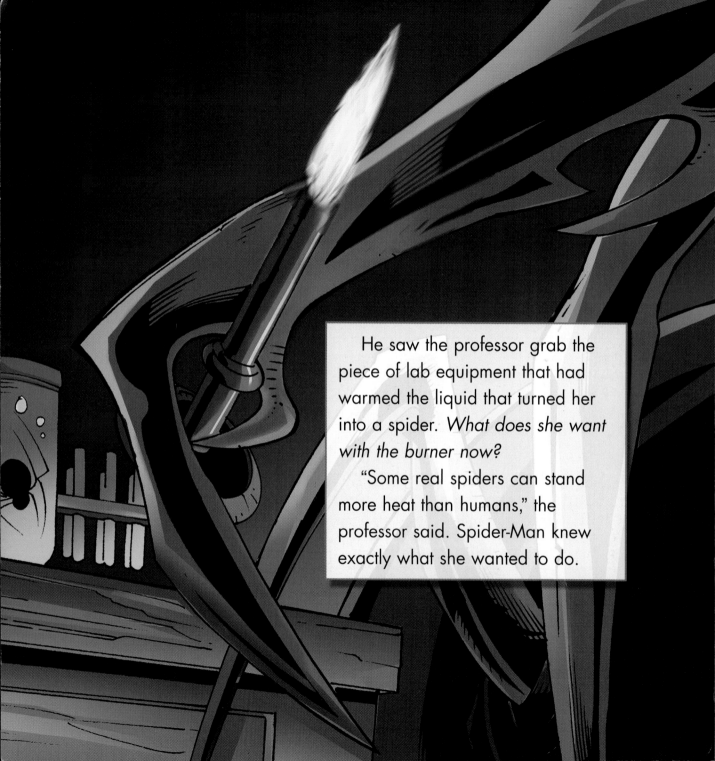

He saw the professor grab the piece of lab equipment that had warmed the liquid that turned her into a spider. *What does she want with the burner now?*

"Some real spiders can stand more heat than humans," the professor said. Spider-Man knew exactly what she wanted to do.

"This will burn you, but it won't hurt me," she screeched. Spider-Man knew that the professor was right. He could feel himself sweating inside his costume as the flame grew bigger and brighter. He looked around for a way out, but he couldn't think of anything.

Spider-Man saw the super-spider turn her eyes away from the flame.

That doesn't make sense, he thought. *The heat doesn't bother her. Why isn't she watching what she's doing?* Then he remembered something the professor had said in class.

The professor had said that some spiders see better in darkness than in light. And the first thing she did as the super-spider was shut the light off.

Spider-Man knew what to do. But did he have time? The flame was coming closer, and the giant spider's legs were squeezing tighter.

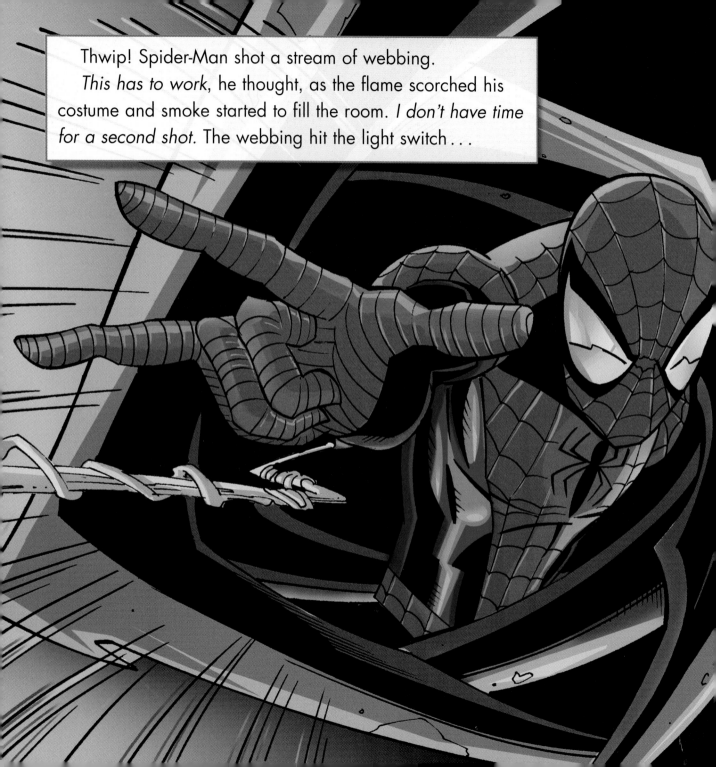

Thwip! Spider-Man shot a stream of webbing.
This has to work, he thought, as the flame scorched his costume and smoke started to fill the room. *I don't have time for a second shot.* The webbing hit the light switch...

...and as the room filled with light, the super-spider squealed and dropped him. *She can't stand so much light!* Spider-Man thought. *But she won't stay down for long. I'll have to move fast.*

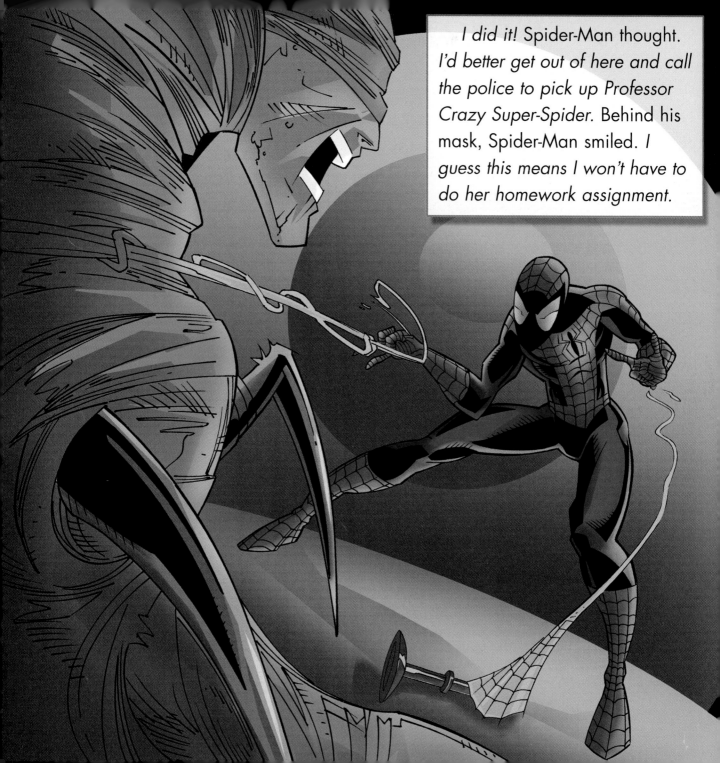

I did it! Spider-Man thought. I'd better get out of here and call the police to pick up Professor Crazy Super-Spider. Behind his mask, Spider-Man smiled. I guess this means I won't have to do her homework assignment.

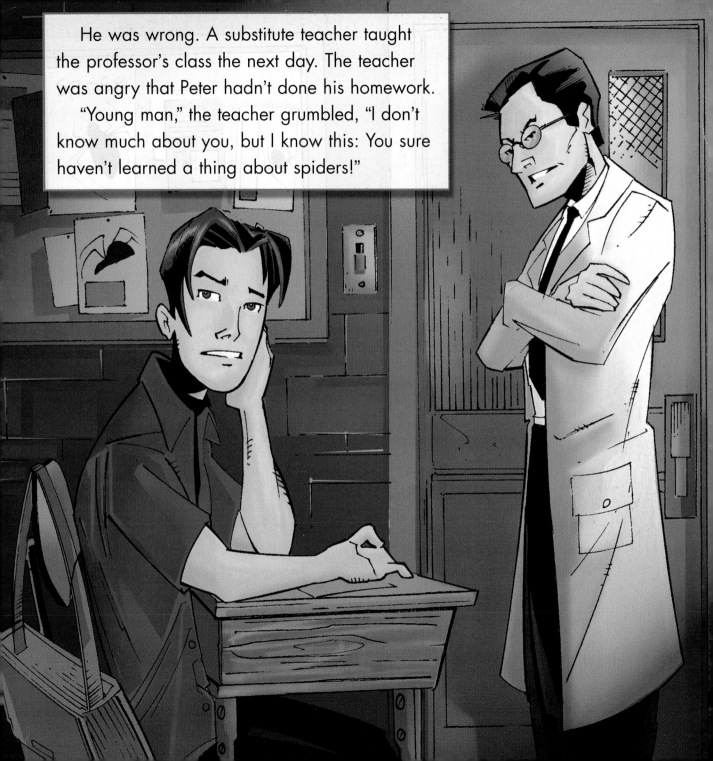

He was wrong. A substitute teacher taught the professor's class the next day. The teacher was angry that Peter hadn't done his homework. "Young man," the teacher grumbled, "I don't know much about you, but I know this: You sure haven't learned a thing about spiders!"

THIS BOOK BELONGS TO:

_____